GHOST ON THE OPEN ROAD

Kenneth Haines
Ghost on the Open Road

Published by Spines Publishing Platform
ISBN: 979-8-89691-512-6

GHOST ON THE OPEN ROAD

KENNETH HAINES

CONTENTS

I

THE ICE-COVERED ROAD

THE ICE-COVERED ROAD is a treacherous stretch that holds stories of both caution and sorrow. Located in a remote area, this road is notorious for sudden weather changes that can turn clear skies into blizzards within moments. For truck drivers, the perilous nature of the ice-covered road is a serious concern, often leading to disastrous consequences. It is a place where many have faced their worst fears, and for one lonely truck driver, it became the setting of an unimaginable fate.

As the driver navigated the icy path, the conditions rapidly deteriorated. Despite years of experience, he felt the familiar pangs of anxiety creeping in as the tires fought for traction against the slick surface. He had been driving through snow storms before, but this particular night was different. The road glistened under the moonlight, creating an illusion of beauty that masked its danger. With each turn, he struggled to maintain control, unaware that the journey would end in tragedy, forever changing his existence.

After the crash, the driver's spirit lingered on the very road that had claimed his life. In this twilight state, he found himself still behind the wheel, a phantom among the living. The realization of his death eluded him for years, as he continued to traverse the familiar highways, oblivious to the fact that he was no longer bound by the physical realm. His truck became a vessel of memories, each mile a reminder of the life he once led, yet he remained trapped in a cycle of endless driving, searching for solace.

The ice-covered road transformed into a haunting landscape, echoing with the remnants of past journeys. Other drivers would occasionally report feeling a chill as they passed through certain sections, often attributing it to the weather. However, for those who were more attuned to the supernatural, the presence of the lonely driver was palpable. They would catch glimpses of his spectral truck, illuminated by the ghostly glow of its headlights, as it glided silently over the icy surface, a poignant reminder of the dangers that lurked within those frozen miles.

2
THE ACCIDENT

THE ICY GRIP of winter had settled heavily across the highways, transforming the once-familiar landscape into a treacherous expanse of white. For many, such conditions called for increased caution, but for one lonely truck driver, the call to deliver his cargo remained paramount. He had spent countless hours on the road, navigating through blizzards and storms, his truck a second home. On that fateful night, as the wind howled and the snow fell like a curtain, he continued his journey, unaware of the dangers that lurked ahead.

As the driver approached a particularly treacherous bend, the weight of his cargo shifted, causing his truck to skid on the ice-covered road. The world around him seemed to slow as he fought for control, his heart racing in tandem with the spiraling truck. The screech of metal against asphalt filled the air, drowning out the howling wind. In a matter of seconds, his life irrevocably changed. The truck careened off the road, crashing into a snowbank, and in an instant, everything went dark. When the driver finally awoke, he found himself in a strange, ethereal place. His truck was still there, but everything around him seemed different. The once-familiar road now felt otherworldly, bathed in a ghostly glow.

3
THE GHOSTLY STATE

As time passed, the lonely driver began to notice other vehicles passing through his icy domain. He watched them struggle against the same treacherous conditions that had led to his demise. Desperate to warn them, he tried to make his presence known. Flickering headlights, eerie whispers in the wind, and fleeting glimpses of his spectral form became his attempts to communicate.

But most drivers brushed off these signs as tricks of the light or their own imagination. Only a few, those sensitive to the supernatural, truly felt his presence. They would see his spectral truck, its headlights glowing eerily in the night, and feel a chill that had nothing to do with the weather.

This fateful night, a young woman named Sarah, an inexperienced truck driver, found herself on the ice-covered road. The ghostly driver sensed her fear and determination. He followed her closely, using his limited ability to influence her journey. Flickering headlights, whispers in the wind, and ghostly apparitions guided her through the treacherous path.

Sarah's journey was fraught with danger, but the ghostly driver's guidance kept her safe. In a climactic moment, she reached the end of the icy stretch, her life intact. The ghostly driver felt a sense of peace, knowing he had prevented another tragedy.

Again it became dark around him, The driver, now aware of his ghostly state, found himself trapped in a perpetual cycle of driving the ice-covered road. Every attempt to escape led him back to the same stretch of highway, the scenery around him constantly shifting yet remaining hauntingly familiar. He watched helplessly as other vehicles passed by, their drivers unseeing and unaware of his plight.

One night, as he drove along the desolate road, he noticed a small car skidding on the ice. The driver, a young woman, struggled to control the vehicle as it spun out of control. Compelled by a deep sense of duty, the ghostly truck driver maneuvered his spectral truck to block the car from sliding off the road. The impact never came, as his truck passed through the car like a phantom, but the sudden distraction caused the young woman to regain control and safely stop her vehicle.

Realizing he still had some power to influence the living, the ghostly driver began to take on a new role as a guardian of the ice-covered road. He watched over the treacherous stretch, using subtle signals to warn drivers of impending danger. Flickering headlights, sudden gusts of wind, and faint whispers in the night became his tools.

Despite his efforts, not all drivers heeded the warnings. Some were too engrossed in their own thoughts, while others dismissed the signs as mere tricks of the mind. Yet, those who were attuned to the supernatural felt his presence and understood the guidance he offered.

Word of the ghostly guardian began to spread among truckers and frequent travelers of the ice-covered road. Stories of near-misses and inexplicable saves circulated, turning the lonely truck driver into a legend. Though many dismissed the tales as folklore, those who had experienced his intervention knew the truth.

One particularly stormy night, the ghostly driver encountered a convoy of trucks struggling through the blizzard. Sensing the danger ahead, he took swift action. He created a series of spectral signals, leading the convoy safely through the treacherous bends and icy patches. The drivers, though unaware of the source of their good fortune, followed the strange lights and made it through the storm unscathed.

After countless nights of guiding and protecting the living, the ghostly driver began to feel a change within himself. The restlessness that had once plagued him started to fade, replaced by a sense of fulfillment. He had found purpose in his spectral existence, a way to atone for his past and protect others from the fate he had suffered.

As dawn broke over the icy landscape, the ghostly driver felt a warmth spread through him. The first rays of sunlight pierced the gloom, illuminating his truck with a golden glow. As the days turned into weeks, the lonely truck driver became acquainted with the other spirits who roamed the highways.

Each ghost carried the weight of their unfinished business, and their stories resonated deeply with him. They shared tales of love and loss, of missed opportunities and unspoken goodbyes. Despite their ethereal existence, a sense of camaraderie formed among them, bound by their shared fate.

The driver learned to navigate the spectral highways, guided by the faint glow of other ghostly vehicles that glided silently beside him. The once-treacherous roads now felt like a bittersweet purgatory, where time seemed to stretch endlessly. The driver listened intently to the stories of his fellow spirits, piecing together the fragments of their past lives and the moments that tethered them to the living world.

4

SEEKING CLOSURE

HAUNTED by the memories of his own life, the driver felt a growing urge to find closure. He longed to reach out to his family, to let them know he was at peace. The other spirits, sensing his need, offered their guidance. Together, they devised a plan to make their presence known to the living, hoping to convey their messages of love and farewell.

One cold, moonlit night, the driver and his ghostly companions gathered at a remote truck stop, a place where the boundary between the living and the dead felt particularly thin. Through a series of spectral signals—flickering lights, whispered words, and mysterious radio interference—they managed to catch the attention of a young truck driver named Sam.

Sam, intrigued and unnerved by the strange occurrences, decided to investigate. As he listened to the ghostly whispers and followed the eerie lights, he gradually pieced together the story of the lonely truck driver and the other lost souls. Moved by their plight, Sam agreed to help convey their messages to the living.

With Sam as their bridge, the spirits found solace in knowing that their stories would be told. The lonely truck driver, in particular, felt a profound sense of relief as Sam promised to deliver his final message to his family. The spectral community watched as Sam drove away, their hopes riding with him.

As dawn broke over the horizon, the ghostly driver felt a shift within himself. The restless longing that had bound him to the highways began to fade, replaced by a sense of peace and fulfillment. The spectral landscape, once a place of endless wandering, now felt like a sanctuary of closure and redemption.

One by one, the spirits found their peace and faded into the light, their unfinished business finally resolved. The lonely truck driver, his mission complete, took one last look at the highways he had haunted. With a sense of gratitude and serenity, he too was ready but something kept holding him back.

5
HOMECOMING

He pulls up to a familiar house, its silhouette etched in his memory. Climbing out of his rig, he looks around and is struck by the eerie silence. There isn't a sound as he walks to the door. When he goes to reach the door handle, his hand passes through it, and he realizes with a start that he can walk through it.

Once inside, he sees dirty dishes still on the table and counter, abandoned in a rush. The house is shrouded in an unnerving quiet. He looks in one room and sees drawers spilled out on the bed, their contents scattered, but there is no sign of life. Moving to another room, he finds it in a similar state—drawers emptied, papers strewn across the floor.

Then, he sees a picture frame lying on the bed. He picks it up, sinking down onto the disheveled sheets. The photo captures a moment of joy: himself with his darling wife and son. Grief-stricken, he begins to cry, the weight of his spectral existence crashing down on him.

The silence around him feels heavier now, filled with the echoes of the life he once had. In that moment of sorrow, he understands the full extent of his fate. His family, his home, everything he held dear, was now lost to him, left behind in the world of the living.

As his tears fall soundlessly onto the bed, the driver is drawn to the memories captured in the photograph. He recalls the laughter and love that once filled the house, now replaced by silence and disarray. The grief and guilt of being unable to protect his family weigh heavily on his spectral heart.

Determined to find out what happened, he roams the house, looking for clues. The scattered papers reveal frantic notes and hastily packed belongings, hinting at a hurried departure. He can almost hear the echoes of his family's last moments in the house—their voices, their fear, their hope.

One particularly poignant discovery is a letter left behind by his wife, addressed to him. Her words, filled with love and sorrow, speak of their struggle to cope with his loss and the desperate decision to leave the house. Reading her words, he feels a renewed sense of purpose. Though he can no longer be with them in life, he can watch over them from the other side.

The driver begins to follow his family's trail, determined to protect them from afar. His journey takes him through the highways and byways, always vigilant, always watching. He influences the living world in subtle ways—turning off lights left on, guiding lost travelers, and warding off dangers.

Despite his ethereal form, the bond with his family remains strong. Their safety and happiness become his sole focus, driving him to learn more about his spectral abilities and the limits of his influence. He becomes an unseen protector, finding peace in his new purpose.

He feels his body being jolted, a sensation that jars him from his spectral existence. He has no idea what is going on, and all he sees are flashes of light and shadow. Disoriented and confused, he struggles to comprehend the sensations that envelop him.

As the flashes continue, he catches glimpses of familiar faces—his wife and son, their expressions filled with concern and hope. The sounds of medical equipment beep in the background, interspersed with urgent voices. He tries to reach out, but his movements feel sluggish, as if he's moving through water.

6
BETWEEN WORLDS

In the midst of the confusion, he starts to piece together what is happening. He is caught between two worlds—one foot in the realm of the living, the other still tethered to his ghostly existence. The jolting sensation is the pull of life trying to reclaim him, to draw him back from the brink.

He struggles to focus, to grasp onto the fragments of reality that flicker in and out of his vision. The faces of his loved ones provide a beacon of hope, guiding him through the haze. As the jolts grow stronger, he feels a surge of determination, an instinctual drive to return to them.

With each jolt, the flashes become clearer, the sounds sharper. He hears the voice of his wife calling out to him, urging him to come back. The warmth of their love permeates the cold, spectral veil that surrounds him. He fights against the pull of the afterlife, fueled by the desire to reunite with his family.

Gradually, the flashes merge into a continuous stream of light, and he finds himself hovering on the edge of consciousness. The ghostly world fades, replaced by the sterile brightness of a hospital room. The beeping of monitors and the murmur of voices grow louder, grounding him in reality.

With a final, forceful jolt, he gasps for air and opens his eyes. The blinding light recedes, and he sees the tear-streaked faces of his wife and son. They rush to his side, their hands gripping his as if to anchor him to the world of the living.

Tears of relief and joy flow freely as they embrace, the weight of his ghostly journey lifting from his shoulders. Though the memories of his spectral existence linger, he knows that he has been given a second chance. The road ahead may be uncertain, but with his family by his side, he feels ready to face whatever lies ahead.

7
STORIES OF OTHER LOST SOULS

In the vast expanse of America's highways, stories of lost souls linger like shadows in the dusk. One such tale is that of a lonely truck driver who met his fate on an ice-covered road. As he navigated the treacherous terrain, the weight of his long hours and solitude bore down on him. In a split second, a moment of inattention led to a catastrophic wreck. However, rather than fading into the void, he found himself still behind the wheel of his rig, unaware that his earthly existence had come to an abrupt end. For him, the road became an eternal journey, a haunting reminder of the life he once lived.

This driver, like many others, became a ghostly figure on the highways he once traversed. His spirit roams the stretches of asphalt, a silent observer of the world he left behind. Fellow truckers often speak of the phantom truck that appears in their rearview mirrors, only to vanish when they glance back. Some describe the feeling of being followed by an unseen presence, a chill that runs down their spine as they drive through desolate stretches of highway. These experiences have cemented his place in the lore of the road, a testament to the enduring spirit of those who lived for the open highway.

Another story echoes through the corridors of abandoned truck stops and rest areas. A driver, who found solace in the solitude of long hauls, fell victim to exhaustion. He succumbed to sleep one fateful night while parked at a deserted rest area, never to wake again. His spirit, restless and searching, now wanders the very stops where he once found refuge. Truckers often report feelings of unease when stopping at these locations, as if they are being watched. The faint sound of a truck idling in the distance can sometimes be heard, but when they investigate, they find nothing but silence and the cold night air.

The highways are also home to the spirit of a female driver who was tragically lost during a storm. Her story is one of longing, as she drove through the rain-soaked roads, desperate to reach her family. After losing control of her vehicle, she perished alone, leaving her loved ones in anguish. Now, her presence can be felt on stormy nights, where her spirit searches for a way home. Truckers who pass through during inclement weather often report seeing a figure in white standing by the roadside, beckoning for help, a reminder of the fragility of life and the connections we hold dear.

These stories of lost souls serve as poignant reminders of the lives once lived on the open road. They are a testament to the struggles and sacrifices of those who dedicated their lives to the journey. The highways, while often seen as mere routes to destinations, are imbued with the echoes of those who traversed them. As truck drivers continue their solitary voyages, they may encounter the spirits of those who came before, reminding them that they are not alone, even in their darkest moments. The tales of these lost souls weave a rich tapestry of history, haunting the highways and ensuring that their memories endure in the hearts and minds of those who travel the open road.

8
THE ROLE OF THE LONELY DRIVER

THE ROLE of the lonely driver in the context of "Ghost on the Open Road" serves as a haunting reminder of the isolation often experienced by those who navigate the long stretches of highway. For many truck drivers, the open road is both a sanctuary and a prison. The vast expanses can evoke feelings of freedom, yet the solitude can become suffocating, especially during long hauls that span days without human interaction. This juxtaposition of liberation and loneliness creates a fertile ground for ghostly encounters and supernatural tales, particularly for those who have faced tragic fates on these desolate paths.

One of the most poignant narratives surrounding the lonely driver is that of a truck driver who met an untimely end on an ice-covered road. This driver, like many, was accustomed to the demands of the job, often pushing through adverse weather conditions out of a sense of duty or financial necessity. The moments leading up to the accident are often described as eerily quiet, with the driver perhaps contemplating the emptiness of the road ahead. After the accident, the transition from life to the afterlife is marked by confusion and an unsettling realization that they are still driving, unaware of their own demise.

This phenomenon raises questions about the nature of existence and the ties that bind individuals to their chosen paths, even in death.

In the spirit world, this lonely driver embodies the essence of those who, despite their physical absence, continue to traverse the highways they once knew. They become spectral figures, haunting the very roads where their lives were cut short. Their presence is often felt by living drivers who report unusual occurrences: the feeling of being watched, sudden temperature drops, or the inexplicable urge to slow down in certain areas. These encounters serve as reminders of the lives that once flowed through these corridors and the stories that linger long after the vehicles have passed.

The phenomenon of the lonely driver also prompts reflection on the psychological aspects of isolation experienced by truckers. Loneliness can lead to a range of emotional and mental health challenges, which may be intensified during long trips. The idea of driving through a ghostly landscape can symbolize the internal struggles faced by many drivers, mirroring their feelings of being lost or disconnected. In this sense, the spirits of lonely drivers may serve as metaphors for the real-life issues confronting those who spend extensive periods alone on the road, emphasizing the need for connection and understanding.

Ultimately, the role of the lonely driver in "Ghost on the Open Road" transcends mere storytelling. It highlights the intersection of life, death, and the human experience on the highways that stretch across the country. As these spirits continue to haunt the roads, they remind us of the fragility of life and the enduring impact of our journeys. The tales of these drivers encourage a deeper appreciation for the stories behind the wheel and the unseen connections that bind us all, reinforcing the notion that even in solitude, we are never truly alone.

9
THE PHANTOM HITCHHIKER

The Phantom Hitchhiker has long been a staple of ghostly lore, captivating the imaginations of travelers and truckers alike. Picture this: a weary driver on a lonely stretch of highway, the sun dipping below the horizon, casting long shadows across the asphalt. As night descends, the headlights illuminate the road ahead, revealing a figure standing at the roadside, thumb outstretched, waiting for a ride. This specter, often dressed in clothing from a bygone era, is both a beacon of intrigue and a harbinger of the unknown. While many dismiss these tales as mere folklore, truckers know there's an air of truth that lingers in these chilling encounters.

As the story goes, our phantom hitchhiker often appears to those who are alone, perhaps seeking companionship on the desolate roads. Truckers, accustomed to the solitude of long hauls, have reported picking up these ethereal travelers only to experience puzzling phenomena. Conversations that feel real yet slip away like mist, sudden cold drafts in the cab, or the eerie sensation of being watched can fill the air with an electrifying tension. These encounters remind us that we share our journeys with more than the living, and that the highways are woven with the threads of both past and present.

The most compelling aspect of these encounters lies in the stories that unfold after the hitchhiker is dropped off. In many accounts, the trucker turns to offer a final glance, only to find the seat empty, as if the ghostly passenger vanished into thin air. Some recount hearing whispered warnings or receiving cryptic messages that resonate deeply long after the encounter. These moments not only spark curiosity but also inspire reflection on the connections we forge, even with those who exist beyond the veil of life. The lessons imparted by these spectral beings often lead to newfound perspectives on mortality and the fleeting nature of existence.

Truckers who have shared their experiences of the Phantom Hitchhiker often speak of a shift in their outlook after these encounters. They emerge from the experience not just as drivers on a highway, but as custodians of stories that bridge the gap between the living and the dead. Each tale adds depth to the tapestry of their profession, reminding them that every mile traveled is a journey through history, filled with echoes of those who have come before. In this way, the phantom hitchhiker serves as a poignant symbol of the interconnectedness of all souls, encouraging us to honor the roads we traverse and the spirits we meet along the way.

In the end, the tales of the Phantom Hitchhiker are an invitation to embrace the mystery of the open road. They encourage truckers and travelers alike to remain open to the unknown, to listen to the whispers of the past, and to acknowledge the presence of those who continue to journey alongside us, even if only in spirit. As each driver navigates their path, they carry the essence of these encounters, woven into the very fabric of their travels, reminding us that the highways are not merely conduits for transport but realms of possibility, where the supernatural coexists with the everyday.

10

THE VANISHING TRUCK STOP

THE VANISHING TRUCK STOP stands as a testament to the mysteries that weave through America's highways, a place where the ordinary meets the extraordinary. Nestled between stretches of asphalt that seem to stretch infinitely, this truck stop appeared as a beacon of hope for weary travelers. It was a haven where truckers could refuel their bodies and souls, sharing stories over steaming cups of coffee at the diner. Yet, it was a place that, for some, would become a haunting memory, an encounter with the inexplicable that would linger long after the engine roared back to life.

Truckers often spoke of the truck stop that would seemingly vanish from their GPS, only to reappear when they were most in need. Those who had experienced it described a sense of urgency that compelled them to seek refuge there, as if an unseen force guided them. The diner's neon lights flickered like a lighthouse in the fog, inviting and warm, yet shrouded in an aura of something otherworldly. It was said that once a trucker parked his rig and stepped inside, he would find himself in a timeless realm, where the clock's hands spun differently, and the chatter of fellow drivers echoed with an eerie familiarity.

Many who entered the diner felt an unshakeable sense of déjà vu, as if they had been there before. The patrons, often clad in denim and leather, shared tales of their own ghostly encounters—stories of lost loves, unfulfilled dreams, and paths taken and not taken. Some claimed that the staff, always smiling and attentive, were not quite of this world. With eyes that sparkled with ancient wisdom, they served up not just meals, but a connection to something far greater, a reminder that every journey is woven with threads of the past. The air buzzed with the energy of shared experiences, a tapestry of lives intersecting for a fleeting moment.

Yet, just as mysteriously as it appeared, The Vanishing Truck Stop would vanish from existence, leaving behind only the faintest memory in the minds of those who had experienced its warmth. Truckers would find themselves searching for the familiar diner, only to drive past empty stretches of road where it once stood. The tales of the vanishing stop became legends among the trucking community, each recounting a personal experience that seemed to defy explanation. Those who had visited often wondered if it was a figment of their imagination or a genuine supernatural encounter, a reminder that the highways were not merely paths to destinations, but gateways to the unknown.

The Vanishing Truck Stop serves as a poignant reminder of the magic that lies just beyond the veil of reality. In the world of trucking, where the distance between dreams and reality can become blurred, it stands as a symbol of connection—between travelers, their journeys, and the ethereal realms that weave through the fabric of existence. For those who believe in the mystical, the truck stop is more than a mere rest area; it is an invitation to explore the unseen, to embrace the stories that linger in the winds of the highway, and to remember that every journey is a sacred path filled with the echoes of those who have traveled before.

II
THE ENCHANTED REST AREA

The Enchanted Rest Area is a place where the mundane meets the mystical, a waypoint on long, winding roads where the weary traveler can pause, stretch, and perhaps encounter something beyond the ordinary. Nestled beneath towering pines and bathed in the soft glow of twilight, this rest area has long been a refuge for truckers and wanderers alike. Those who stop here often speak of an inexplicable energy that seems to linger in the air, a serene presence that invites reflection and connection with the unseen.

As truckers pull into the rest area, they may be greeted by the soothing sounds of rustling leaves and the distant call of night creatures. Many have reported strange occurrences: flickering lights that dance in the corners of their vision, shadows that appear to move with intent, or the sensation of being watched by friendly eyes. It is a space where stories intertwine, and the air is thick with the tales of those who have come before, each leaving their mark on the enchanted ground.

One of the most captivating legends surrounding the rest area involves a spectral figure known as the Highway Guardian. Truckers claim to have seen this kind-hearted apparition, a woman dressed in vintage clothing, who appears when someone is in distress or facing danger. She is said to guide lost souls back to safety, offering comfort in the form of gentle whispers and warm smiles. Her presence has been felt during moments of uncertainty, reminding those who pass through that they are never truly alone on their journeys.

As the sun dips below the horizon, the rest area transforms into a canvas of possibilities. Campfires may flicker to life as weary travelers gather to share their own ghostly encounters and the lessons learned along the way. Each story is woven with threads of hope, resilience, and a touch of magic, proving that every journey can hold something extraordinary. These moments of connection create a tapestry of shared experiences, binding the truckers together through the mysteries of the road.

The Enchanted Rest Area stands as a testament to the belief that the highways we travel are not merely stretches of asphalt, but portals to the unknown. It invites all who stop to open their hearts and minds to the wonders that lie just beyond the veils of reality. For those willing to listen closely, the whispers of the past and the promise of the future echo through the trees, reminding us that every journey is a chance to embrace the magic that surrounds us.

12
CURSED LANDMARKS AND THEIR STORIES

CURSED landmarks dot the highways of America, each with a tale steeped in mystery and a history rich in the supernatural. These sites, often overlooked by the hurried traveler, invite those with a sense of adventure and a belief in the unknown. The stories that surround these locations can send shivers down the spine, yet they also inspire a deeper understanding of the connection between the past and present. For truckers who traverse these routes, the legends of cursed landmarks serve as reminders of the roads traveled and the history etched into the very asphalt beneath their wheels.

One such landmark is the infamous "Dead Man's Curve," a treacherous bend that has claimed countless lives over the years. Truckers often recount tales of phantom hitchhikers appearing at the curve, only to vanish without a trace. These spectral figures serve as a chilling reminder of the dangers that lurk on the open road. Yet, amidst the fear, there lies an invitation to honor those who have lost their lives; a chance for reflection on the fragility of life and the importance of safe travels. Each time a trucker passes this curve, they become part of an ongoing story, a cycle of remembrance and caution woven into the fabric of the highway.

Another notable cursed landmark is the abandoned bridge known as "Whistler's Bridge." Travelers have reported hearing eerie whispers and strange sounds emanating from the structure, especially at dusk. Legends tell of a tragic accident that occurred on the bridge, leading to the belief that the spirits of those lost still linger. For those brave enough to stop and listen, the whispers can feel like a conversation with the past, urging them to acknowledge the history that resides in the shadows. This connection between the present and the lost souls of yesteryear serves to remind us that every journey is interwoven with stories waiting to be discovered.

For the intrepid trucker, these cursed landmarks also symbolize resilience. The tales of the past serve as a testament to human endurance against adversity and the importance of remembrance. Each story offers a lesson, whether it's about the importance of caution, the weight of history, or simply the acknowledgment of those who came before. As truckers share their experiences, they weave a tapestry of narratives that enrich the culture of the open road, transforming potential fear into inspiration. Each mile traveled becomes a tribute to the lives intertwined with these landmarks, encouraging a deeper appreciation for the journey itself.

As we navigate the highways, we are not just passing through; we are part of a larger narrative that spans generations. The cursed landmarks remind us that the road is alive with stories, haunted by the echoes of those who have journeyed before us. Embracing these tales invites us to explore the supernatural elements of our travels and fosters a sense of connection to the past. For every trucker who dares to pause and reflect, there lies the opportunity to not only confront the ghosts of the road but also to honor the enduring spirit of adventure that defines each journey taken.

13
THE GHOSTLY DISPATCHER

THE NIGHT WAS as dark as the open highway could get, with only the faint glow of the moon illuminating the endless stretch of asphalt. Long-haul truckers often speak of the strange encounters that accompany their solitary journeys, but none is as hauntingly captivating as the tale of the Ghostly Dispatcher. This ethereal figure is said to appear at truck stops and rest areas, providing guidance and warnings to weary drivers who have lost their way. As the stories go, those who heed the dispatcher's advice are often led safely through treacherous conditions, while those who dismiss the spectral presence may find themselves facing dire consequences.

The Ghostly Dispatcher is often described as a shadowy figure, clad in a vintage trucker's cap and a weathered leather jacket, reminiscent of a bygone era when trucking was a nomadic adventure. Drivers recount how this spirit appears just as they feel the weight of exhaustion settling in, illuminating the darkness with a gentle, otherworldly glow. The dispatcher's voice, soft yet commanding, carries the wisdom of countless miles traveled, guiding the lost souls of the highway back to safety. This connection to the past serves as a reminder of the sacrifices made by generations of truckers, their spirits forever entwined with the roads they traveled.

Many truckers share stories of uncanny encounters with the dispatcher, often during moments of vulnerability on their long hauls. One driver, after hours of driving through a relentless storm, recalls pulling into a dimly lit rest area. Feeling overwhelmed and uncertain, he spotted the ghostly figure leaning against a weathered truck, exuding an aura of calm. The dispatcher offered a few words of encouragement before pointing toward a hidden route that would bypass the worst of the storm. With gratitude in his heart, the driver followed the spectral advice and emerged from the tempest unscathed, forever thankful for the supernatural intervention.

Further tales weave a rich tapestry of the dispatcher's role as a protector, a beacon of hope for those navigating the lonely roads. Some drivers report hearing the faint sound of a truck engine revving in the distance, only to find the dispatcher waiting at the next rest stop, ready to offer advice tailored to their specific journey. These encounters often inspire truckers to share their own stories of resilience and camaraderie, strengthening the bonds within the trucking community. The ghostly presence becomes a symbol of solidarity, reminding drivers that they are never truly alone on the vast highways.

As stories of the Ghostly Dispatcher circulate among truckers, they serve as both cautionary tales and sources of inspiration. The legend embodies the spirit of the open road, blending mysticism with the everyday realities of those who traverse the highways. In a world where the journey can be filled with uncertainty, the dispatcher's ghostly presence offers solace and reassurance. For many, these encounters transcend mere folklore, becoming a testament to the enduring connection between the living and the departed, reminding us all that the road is not just a path to a destination, but a journey filled with stories waiting to be told.

14
THE REST STOP WITH A DARK PAST

THE ROADSIDE REST STOP, nestled between stretches of endless asphalt and flickering neon lights, has long been a sanctuary for weary travelers. However, this particular rest stop carries with it an unsettling history that lingers in the air like a fog. Truckers often share tales of strange occurrences, whispers of a time when the stop served as a refuge for those seeking solace, only to be met with shadows of sorrow. It stands as a reminder that not all places of rest are mere havens; some are steeped in the echoes of the past, waiting to tell their stories to those who dare to listen.

Legend has it that many moons ago, this stop was the site of a tragic accident, where a trucker lost control on a rain-slick road and collided with a barrier. The driver, a beloved figure in the local trucking community, was known for his kindness and generosity. Ever since that fateful night, his spirit has been said to wander the rest area, seeking to provide comfort to fellow drivers. Those who have encountered him often speak of a warm breeze that sweeps through the area, accompanied by the faint scent of his favorite cologne, as if he is there to remind them that they are never truly alone on their journeys.

As the sun sets and darkness envelops the highway, the rest stop transforms into a realm where the veil between the living and the departed grows thin. Truckers recount stories of their experiences at the stop, where they have felt inexplicable sensations—an unseen hand resting on their shoulder or a whisper in their ear urging them to drive safely. These encounters are not to be dismissed as mere figments of exhaustion; rather, they serve as poignant reminders of the bonds formed on the open road and the care that transcends the physical realm. Each tale shared becomes a thread in the tapestry of the trucking community, weaving together the supernatural and the everyday.

The rest stop also holds a unique allure for those drawn to the paranormal. Ghost hunters and curious souls alike visit, hoping to capture evidence of the ethereal presence that many claim to feel. From strange lights flickering in the distance to the sound of phantom footsteps echoing across the pavement, each visit offers a chance to connect with something beyond the ordinary. It is a place where stories intertwine, where the past collides with the present, and where the whispers of lost souls remind us of the fragility of life and the importance of cherishing every moment on our journeys.

In the end, the rest stop with a dark past is more than just a place to stretch one's legs; it is a testament to the enduring spirit of those who have traveled the highways before us. Each encounter, each whisper, serves as an invitation to reflect on our own lives and the paths we choose. As truckers continue to share their stories, they keep the memory of the lost alive, ensuring that no one is forgotten. In the quiet moments at the rest stop, amidst the laughter and camaraderie, there lies a profound sense of connection—a reminder that we are all part of a larger story, united by the open road and the mysteries it holds.

15
SIGNS FROM BEYOND

In the vast stretches of open road, where the horizon meets the sky, many truckers have shared tales of inexplicable signs from beyond. These experiences often transcend the mundane, offering glimpses into a world that defies logic and invites wonder. As the engine hums and the tires roll across asphalt, drivers find themselves not just in the realm of the physical but also in a space where the ethereal can make its presence known. Whether it's a flickering sign that seems to flash with purpose or an unexpected vision on the roadside, these occurrences serve as reminders that we are never truly alone on our journeys.

One of the most common signs reported by truckers involves the sudden appearance of ghostly figures along desolate highways. These silhouettes often seem to beckon or guide, leading drivers to safety or revealing something significant about their journeys. Some have recounted experiences where they felt an unseen hand guiding them through treacherous weather conditions or steering them away from potential accidents. These mystical encounters instill a sense of purpose and connection, suggesting that the spirits of those who once traveled these roads may still be watching over us, offering protection and wisdom to those in need.

Highway rest stops have also become locations of supernatural happenings, where truckers and travelers alike have reported strange occurrences. It is not uncommon for a weary driver to feel a sudden chill or hear whispers in the wind while taking a break. Many have shared stories of finding notes or tokens left behind, seemingly by invisible hands, carrying messages of hope or encouragement. These moments serve as gentle nudges from the universe, urging individuals to stay the course and trust in their own journeys. The rest stops become portals of connection, where the past and present blend, reminding us of the many souls who have traversed the same paths.

The legends surrounding certain highways only add to the intrigue of these signs from beyond. Many routes have become etched in lore, with tales of spectral hitchhikers or phantom vehicles that appear out of nowhere. These stories, passed down through generations of truckers, inspire a sense of camaraderie as drivers share their own encounters. The warmth of shared experiences fosters a community where the extraordinary becomes a part of everyday life. The roads become not just pathways between destinations but conduits of connection to the mysteries that lie just beyond our perception.

Ultimately, these signs from beyond encourage us to remain open to the possibilities that exist in our world. As we navigate the highways of life, we are reminded that every turn may bring us closer to something greater than ourselves. Whether it's a fleeting glimpse of a ghostly figure or an inexplicable feeling of reassurance, these experiences enrich our journeys and inspire us to seek the extraordinary in the ordinary. Embracing the unknown allows us to forge deeper connections not only with the road but also with the stories of those who have traveled before us, reminding us that the spirit of adventure is alive and well, forever guiding us along our ghostly highways.

16

THE WATCHFUL EYES OF THE LOST

THE WINDING ROADS that stretch across the American landscape often conceal more than just the promise of a destination. For truckers, these highways become a tapestry woven with tales of encounters that defy explanation. Among these stories, there exists a recurring theme: the watchful eyes of the lost. These spectral observers are said to linger at the edges of the road, their presence both unsettling and strangely comforting, as if they are guardians of the journeys taken by those who traverse the open highways.

Many truckers share their experiences of feeling an inexplicable gaze upon them during long hours spent driving through the night. It's as if the very spirit of the road awakens, revealing a hidden world that exists alongside the physical realm. Some recount the sensation of being watched when they pass through desolate stretches of highway, where the silence is profound and the darkness feels alive. These moments can evoke a profound sense of connection, urging the drivers to reflect on their own lives, the paths they've chosen, and the souls of those who may have traveled before them.

One particularly famous tale comes from a trucker who frequently navigated the lonely highways of the Midwest. He often felt a strange pull toward a specific stretch of road known for its tragic history. As he drove through the area late one night, he noticed a figure standing by the roadside. The figure appeared to be a woman in a vintage dress, her eyes fixed on his truck with an intensity that sent chills down his spine. Despite the fear that gripped him, he felt compelled to slow down and gaze into her eyes. In that fleeting moment, he sensed a story yearning to be told, a life that had been cut short, yet still lingered in search of understanding.

The watchful eyes of the lost serve as reminders of the many lives intertwined with the highways we travel. Truckers often carry the weight of their own stories, but they also become conduits for the tales of others. Each encounter with these spectral figures opens a portal to shared histories, urging drivers to honor the past even as they forge ahead. It's a poignant reminder that every mile traveled is not just a distance covered but a journey through a landscape rich with the memories and spirits of those who came before.

In the end, the watchful eyes of the lost are not merely haunting apparitions; they embody the spirit of the road itself. For those who embrace the mystical side of their travels, these encounters can inspire a deeper appreciation for the journey and the connections formed along the way. As truckers navigate the vast expanses of the highways, they are reminded that they are never truly alone. The spirits of the lost watch over them, guiding their path and whispering stories from beyond, transforming each trip into a sacred pilgrimage through the unseen realms.

17

THE OLD ROUTE 66 GHOSTS

THE OLD ROUTE 66, often hailed as the "Main Street of America," weaves a tapestry of rich history and nostalgia, but it also serves as a conduit for the spectral and the strange. As truckers traverse this iconic highway, tales of ghostly encounters and eerie happenings abound, weaving a narrative that transcends time. The spirit of the road invites adventurers and weary travelers alike to pause and reflect on the stories that linger just beyond the veil of the visible world. Each mile traveled holds the promise of a mystical encounter, reminding us that the past is never truly gone, but rather exists in a parallel realm, waiting to share its secrets.

One of the most famous ghost stories along Route 66 revolves around the ghost of a young woman known as "The Blue Lady." Legend has it that she met a tragic fate on a lonely stretch of the highway, forever bound to the road where her life was cut short. Truckers often report seeing her apparition, dressed in a flowing blue gown, wandering near abandoned motels and diners. Her presence is said to evoke a sense of melancholy, as she seeks solace from the world that moved on without her. Those who have encountered her spirit often feel compelled to offer her a moment of kindness, a reminder that the power of empathy remains alive, even in the most desolate places.

Further down the road, the ghostly tales grow richer with each passing town. In places like Santa Monica and Springfield, truckers share stories of phantom hitchhikers who appear only to vanish when approached. These spectral figures often embody the lost souls of travelers from decades past, their stories lingering like echoes in the wind. Each encounter serves as a poignant reminder of the lives that once traversed these highways, urging us to honor their journeys while acknowledging the transient nature of our own paths. The road thus becomes a sacred space where past and present converge, offering moments of reflection for those brave enough to listen.

The ghosts of Route 66 also manifest in the form of haunted diners and roadside attractions, where the energy of countless travelers has left an indelible mark. In these establishments, the clatter of dishes and the laughter of patrons often intertwine with whispers of the supernatural. Truckers recount tales of flickering lights, cold spots, and the faint melodies of music from eras long gone. These experiences remind us that the heart of the highway beats not just in the asphalt beneath our tires, but in the memories and spirits of those who have shared a meal, a laugh, or a moment of companionship along the way.

As we journey along the storied Route 66, we find that the ghosts we encounter are not merely phantoms; they are embodiments of the human experience. Each spectral figure and haunting tale invites us to reflect on our own lives and the connections we forge with others. The highway calls us to honor the past while embracing the present, reminding us that our travels are woven into the broader narrative of existence. In this realm of mystical encounters, the ghosts of Route 66 serve as guides, encouraging us to explore the depths of our own stories as we traverse the open road, forever seeking the extraordinary in the ordinary.

18
STORIES FROM THE APPALACHIAN TRAILS

THE APPALACHIAN TRAILS, winding through the heart of the eastern United States, are not just a feast for the eyes; they are a canvas of stories waiting to be told. As truckers navigate these scenic byways, they often find themselves drawn into the realm of the supernatural, where the whispers of the past echo through the towering trees and misty mountains. Each mile traveled on these winding roads is steeped in history, and with that history comes the unexplainable. Truckers have long shared tales of ghostly encounters, mysterious apparitions, and inexplicable phenomena that have occurred during their late-night hauls through these rugged landscapes.

One notable tale involves a seasoned trucker named Hank, who encountered a spectral figure while driving through the dense fog near the Blue Ridge Parkway. As he rounded a bend, a woman in white appeared on the side of the road, her ethereal form almost shimmering in the dim light of his headlights. Hank, accustomed to the challenges of the road, felt an inexplicable urge to stop. As he pulled over, the apparition vanished, leaving behind only a lingering chill in the air. Hank later learned of the local legend of the "White Lady," said to roam the area searching for her lost love. The experience left him questioning the boundary between reality and the supernatural, igniting a sense of wonder that would accompany him on every journey thereafter.

Another haunting story comes from a young trucker named Lisa, who found herself driving late at night through the winding roads of West Virginia. As she passed an old, abandoned gas station, she noticed a flickering light inside. Curious, she pulled over, only to find the station empty and long forgotten. Suddenly, she felt a presence beside her, a gentle whisper urging her to leave. Trusting her instincts, Lisa quickly got back in her truck and drove away, heart racing. Later, she learned of the tragic accident that had claimed the lives of the last owners of the station, their spirits said to linger, protecting travelers from the dangers of the road. This encounter transformed Lisa's perception of her journeys, reminding her that the past can intersect with the present in the most unexpected ways.

The Appalachian Trails are also home to the tale of the Phantom Truck, a ghostly rig that roams the highways, driven by an unseen force. Truckers have reported seeing this spectral vehicle in their rearview mirrors, only for it to vanish when they glance back. Some believe it to be the spirit of a long-lost driver, eternally navigating the roads they once traveled. This legend serves as a reminder of the camaraderie among truckers, who often share the road with both the living and the dead. The Phantom Truck symbolizes the shared journey of those who traverse these haunting highways, connecting them to the stories of those who have come before.

As these stories weave together, they become more than mere folklore; they are a testament to the enduring spirit of the Appalachian Trails. Each encounter offers a glimpse into the mysteries that lie just beyond the veil of the everyday world. For truckers, these supernatural experiences transform their journeys into something magical, reminding them that the road is not just a path to their destination but a bridge to the stories of those who have traveled it before. The Appalachian Trails beckon with whispers of history, inviting all who dare to listen to join in the timeless dance between the living and the spirits that roam the highways of the past.

19
THE MYSTERIOUS FOG

As the sun dipped below the horizon, casting a golden hue across the endless stretch of asphalt, a peculiar fog rolled in from nowhere. It enveloped the highway, transforming the familiar landscape into an eerie, otherworldly realm. Truckers have long whispered about this phenomenon, sharing tales of the mysterious fog that appears without warning, shrouding the road in an ethereal blanket that seems to have a life of its own. This fog is not just a meteorological event; it is a harbinger of the supernatural, a gateway to encounters that linger long after the last mile has been driven.

Many drivers have reported feeling an inexplicable pull toward the fog when it descends. It is as if the mist beckons them to venture deeper into its embrace. Some have described it as a soft, almost inviting presence, while others have felt a chill that runs deeper than the coolness of the air. As they drive through, the world around them fades, and the only sound that remains is the rhythmic hum of their tires against the pavement. In these moments, the line between reality and the otherworldly blurs, and the highway transforms into a place where anything can happen.

Stories abound of phantom hitchhikers appearing in the fog, their figures barely visible until the last moment. Truckers have shared chilling accounts of glancing in their rearview mirrors to find a figure sitting silently in the backseat, only to vanish when they turn around. These apparitions often carry messages of warning or tales of lost journeys, reminding those who encounter them of the fragility of life on the open road. Each story is a thread woven into the fabric of highway lore, creating a tapestry of the unknown that fuels the imagination of all who brave the routes.

The fog has also been known to reveal glimpses of the past, transporting drivers to moments long gone. A trucker once recounted a surreal experience where the mist enveloped him, and he found himself driving through a scene from decades earlier—old gas stations, vintage cars, and the laughter of children playing by the roadside. Such encounters evoke a sense of nostalgia and connection to a time when life seemed simpler, yet they also serve as reminders that the road is haunted by memories, both joyful and sorrowful, that refuse to fade away.

As the fog lifts and the road reappears, those who have traversed its depths carry with them not just a story, but a profound sense of wonder. They are reminded that the highway is more than just a path between destinations; it is a living entity that holds the secrets of the past and the whispers of the unknown. Embracing these ghostly encounters enriches the journey, transforming the mundane into the extraordinary. The mysterious fog serves as a reminder that the open road is filled with possibilities, urging us all to remain open to the wonders that lie just beyond the veil of the familiar.

20
ANIMALS AS MESSENGERS

THROUGHOUT HISTORY, animals have been revered as messengers, harbingers of change, and symbols of the unknown. Truckers, often navigating the vast stretches of America's highways, have their own tales of encounters with animals that seem to transcend the ordinary. These experiences are not just fleeting moments; they become profound connections that challenge our understanding of life, death, and what may lie beyond. As trucks rumble through the night, the flickering headlights illuminate more than just the road ahead; they sometimes reveal the presence of otherworldly guides.

Consider the tale of a weary trucker who, after driving for hours through a desolate stretch of highway, was startled by a deer leaping across the road. Its sudden appearance caused him to slam on the brakes, narrowly avoiding a dangerous collision. Moments later, he saw the deer standing still, its eyes glowing in the darkness. In that instant, he felt an overwhelming sense of calm wash over him, as if the creature had crossed his path to warn him of impending danger. This deer, a symbol of grace and intuition, became a messenger of protection, reminding the driver to remain vigilant and aware of his surroundings.

In another story, a group of truckers gathered at a roadside diner shared their eerie experiences with owls. They spoke of nights when the sound of hooting echoed through the pines, coinciding with significant changes in their lives. One trucker recounted how an owl perched on a signpost seemed to beckon him to take a different route, leading him to an unexpected reunion with an old friend. The owl, often associated with wisdom and transition, served as a guide, steering him toward a path of reconnection and joy. These encounters illustrate how animals can bridge the gap between the physical and spiritual realms, offering guidance when we need it most.

As night descends and the stars twinkle above, the highways become a tapestry of stories woven with the threads of human experience and animal encounters. Many truckers have reported seeing coyotes or foxes appear before them, often at crucial moments in their journeys. These creatures, symbols of cunning and adaptability, remind drivers to embrace change and stay alert. The fleeting glimpses of these animals serve as powerful reminders of the wildness that still exists along the highways, whispering secrets of survival and resilience to those who are willing to listen.

The theme of animals as messengers resonates deeply within the trucking community, where the open road often feels like a liminal space, a threshold between the known and the unknown. Each encounter speaks to the intuition that lies within us all, urging us to trust our instincts. Whether it's a hawk soaring overhead or a dog crossing the road, these moments encourage truckers to pause, reflect, and consider the deeper meanings behind their journeys. In a world that often feels chaotic, these animal encounters provide a sense of grounding, a reminder that nature is constantly communicating, offering wisdom to those who are open to receiving it.

As we traverse the ghostly highways, we come to understand that the stories of animals as messengers are not merely folklore; they are living narratives that connect us to something greater. Each encounter holds the potential to enlighten, heal, and inspire, urging us to recognize the sacredness in the mundane. For truckers, these experiences become part of the tapestry of their travels, enriching their journeys with layers of meaning and reminding them that they are never truly alone on the road. The highways may be long and winding, but they are also alive with the whispers of the wild, guiding us home in ways we may not yet fully comprehend.

21
HONORING THOSE WHO HAUNT

In the realm of the open road, where asphalt stretches endlessly and the horizon beckons, truckers often find themselves crisscrossing through landscapes steeped in history and mystery. Along these highways, stories of the supernatural weave themselves into the very fabric of the journeys taken. Honoring those who haunt is not merely a tribute to the spirits that linger in the shadows; it is an acknowledgment of the profound connections between the living and the departed. These encounters remind us that our travels are not solitary but shared with those who have come before us, whose stories continue to resonate in the solitude of night.

Each highway has its whispers, tales of restless souls whose journeys were cut short or whose passions remain unfulfilled. From the spectral hitchhiker waiting at the roadside to the ghostly trucker who guides weary travelers through treacherous stretches, these figures serve as reminders of the lives that once traversed these paths. They are more than mere legends; they embody the memories of those who loved, laughed, and lived along these very routes. As truckers share their experiences, they keep these stories alive, ensuring that the legacy of those who haunt is honored and remembered.

In many cultures, the act of honoring the dead is a sacred practice. Truckers, in their transient lifestyle, often adopt these customs, creating rituals that acknowledge the spirits they encounter. Whether it's leaving a small token at a rest stop or sharing a story around a campfire, these gestures foster a sense of community between the living and the departed. Every encounter is an opportunity to reflect on the lives of others, to consider their journeys, and to appreciate the impact they have had on the very roads we travel. Through these acts, truckers can find solace, knowing they are part of a larger narrative that transcends time.

The stories of those who haunt the highways are filled with lessons and insights. They speak of caution on lonely stretches, the importance of connection, and the power of storytelling itself. Each tale, whether it sparks fear or inspires wonder, serves as a guidepost for the living. They remind us to be aware of our surroundings, to honor the past, and to cherish the fleeting moments we have with one another. In this way, the spirits of the highways become our teachers, urging us to embrace empathy and understanding as we navigate the complexities of life on the road.

Ultimately, honoring those who haunt is an invitation to celebrate the interplay between life and death, presence and absence. It encourages truckers and all who travel these roads to look beyond the physical realm and recognize the spiritual connections that exist. As highways stretch into the unknown, they carry with them the echoes of countless stories waiting to be told. By honoring these spirits, we not only preserve their memories but also enrich our own journeys, reminding ourselves that every mile traveled is a testament to the resilience of the human spirit and the enduring power of connection, both seen and unseen.

22
SHARING STORIES: A TRUCKER'S BOND

In the heart of America's vast highways, where the asphalt stretches endlessly and the horizon melds with the sky, truckers forge a unique bond that transcends mere camaraderie. It is a connection built not only on shared routes and late-night pit stops but also on the stories that emerge from the shadows of the road. Every driver has a tale waiting to be told, often steeped in the mystical and the supernatural, drawing from the rich tapestry of experiences that accompany life on the open road. These stories, shared in the quiet moments of rest or the vibrant exchanges at truck stops, become the lifeblood of the trucking community, weaving together a narrative that is both personal and collective.

When night falls and the world dims, the highways transform into a canvas for the extraordinary. Truckers often find themselves crossing paths with the inexplicable, encountering apparitions, ethereal lights, and whispers carried by the wind. A driver might recount a chilling encounter with a ghostly hitchhiker who vanished before their eyes or the inexplicable feeling of being watched as they traversed an abandoned stretch of road. These encounters, while unnerving, create a sense of wonder and connection, reminding truckers that they are part of something larger than themselves, a shared experience that binds them to the mysteries of the road.

As stories are exchanged, they serve not just as entertainment but as a source of inspiration and reassurance. Truckers find solace in knowing that others have faced the same eerie moments, that they are not alone in their encounters with the unknown. These tales become a form of folklore, passed down through generations of drivers who share not only their triumphs and trials but also the inexplicable events that have shaped their journeys. In sharing these experiences, they lift one another's spirits and instill a sense of courage to continue navigating the highways, no matter what surprises may await.

The bonds formed through these shared stories often extend beyond the road. Truckers create a community where vulnerability is welcomed, allowing them to confront fears and embrace the supernatural aspects of their travels. Each narrative exchanged fosters understanding and empathy, transforming the loneliness of the long haul into a collective experience. They celebrate the mysteries that accompany their journeys, finding beauty in the stories that linger long after the engine has cooled and the cab falls silent.

Ultimately, the act of sharing stories elevates the trucking experience to something profound. It transforms mundane moments into cherished memories, where the line between reality and the supernatural blurs, creating a rich tapestry of human experience. Through these bonds forged in storytelling, truckers not only navigate the physical roads but also traverse the unexplored territories of the spirit, reminding us all that the journey is not just about the destination, but also about the stories we gather along the way. In the echoes of laughter, the thrill of fear, and the warmth of shared humanity, the trucking community finds its strength, united by the mysteries that haunt their highways.

23
EMBRACING THE UNKNOWN

EMBRACING the unknown is an essential part of the trucker's journey, a call to adventure that resonates deeply with those who traverse the vast, winding highways of America. Each mile traveled opens a door to experiences that extend far beyond the physical road, inviting encounters with the mysterious and the supernatural. The moments that lie outside the realm of the ordinary often become the most cherished stories, weaving a rich tapestry of the mystical that fuels the spirit of every trucker willing to embrace the unexpected.

As the sun dips below the horizon, casting shadows that dance across the asphalt, the road transforms into a portal of possibilities. Truckers often find themselves in remote stretches of highway, where the veil between the earthly realm and the spirit world thins. It is in these twilight hours that the stories come alive—tales of hitchhikers who vanish without a trace, ghostly apparitions guiding weary travelers, and echoes of laughter from long-forgotten souls. Embracing these encounters allows truckers to connect with something greater than themselves, offering a sense of wonder that defies explanation.

The allure of the unknown is not just about the thrill of the supernatural; it is also about the lessons learned along the way. Each ghostly encounter serves as a reminder of the stories that history holds and the lives that once traveled these same roads. When truckers pause to listen to the whispers of the past, they gain insight into their own journeys, learning to navigate their paths with a deeper understanding of courage and resilience. These moments become fuel for the soul, igniting a passion for exploration and a desire to uncover the hidden narratives that lie just beneath the surface.

In embracing the unknown, truckers also cultivate a profound sense of camaraderie within their community. Sharing tales of eerie encounters and unexplainable events fosters connections among those who spend countless hours on the road. The stories become a bridge, linking generations of truckers who have encountered the same ghostly phenomena. It is through the sharing of these experiences that individuals find solace and strength, realizing they are not alone on their journey. Together, they create a collective memory that honors the mysteries and legends of the highways.

Ultimately, embracing the unknown is about opening one's heart and mind to the infinite possibilities that lie ahead. It encourages truckers to venture off the beaten path, to seek out the extraordinary in the everyday, and to welcome the unseen forces that guide them. The road may be filled with uncertainty, but it is precisely in that uncertainty that the magic of the journey unfolds. By allowing themselves to be open to the supernatural, truckers not only enrich their own lives but also contribute to the ever-evolving narrative of the highways they traverse, ensuring that the legends of the road will continue to inspire future generations.

24
THE ROAD AHEAD: HOPE AND MYSTIQUE

THE JOURNEY ahead on the open highways is filled with both uncertainty and promise, a blend of adventure and the supernatural that captivates the hearts of truckers and travelers alike. As the sun dips below the horizon, casting a warm glow across the asphalt, stories of mystical encounters linger in the air like the scent of fresh rain. These tales, shared by weary drivers during rest stops or over cups of coffee in dimly lit diners, serve as reminders that the road is not merely a passage from one destination to another but a realm where the extraordinary can unfold.

Hope thrives in the stories of those who have traveled these highways, where the mundane meets the mystical. Truckers have long been the guardians of these narratives, each twist and turn of the road revealing secrets that defy the ordinary. The whisper of a ghostly figure standing at the roadside, the flicker of lights in the rearview mirror that vanish upon a glance, and the inexplicable feelings of being watched are threads woven into the fabric of their experiences. These encounters instill a sense of wonder, igniting the imagination and reminding us that there is much more to life than what meets the eye.

Mystique envelops the highways, transforming them into corridors of possibility. The legends passed down through generations evoke a sense of connection to those who have come before us, fueling our collective curiosity. As truckers roll through small towns and forgotten stretches of road, they carry with them the weight of these stories, breathing life into the legends that define the American landscape. Whether it's the ghost of a long-lost driver or the spirit of a woman searching for her way home, each tale enriches the journey, creating a tapestry of experiences that bonds travelers across time.

The allure of the unknown beckons us all to embrace the journey ahead, to venture beyond our comfort zones and welcome the supernatural with open arms. Each highway is a promise of adventure, and each mile is an invitation to discover something extraordinary. The road may be unpredictable, but therein lies its beauty. It teaches us resilience and fortitude, encouraging us to find hope in the shadows and joy in the unexpected. As we navigate through this mystical landscape, we learn to listen to the whispers of the road, allowing them to guide our hearts and fuel our spirits.

As we continue to traverse these ghostly highways, let us carry with us the stories of hope and mystique that have shaped our journeys. Each encounter serves as a reminder that we are part of something larger—an ever-evolving narrative that connects us to the past while propelling us into the future. The road ahead is not just about reaching our destinations; it is about embracing the experiences that await us, cherishing the moments of wonder, and believing that the supernatural can coexist with the mundane. In doing so, we unlock the true magic of the open road, where every mile traveled holds the potential for enlightenment and transformation.

Thanks to the Truckers who witnessed their own fate and were able to keep these tales alive for generations to hear and respoken to the next generation. Safe Travels to anyone driving, God Bless you all.

Also by Kenneth Haines

A TALE OF ESCAPE

A group of Earthlings, including a young woman named Elara, is abducted by an invisible alien ship to become part of a cosmic exhibition. Facing the reality of being observed by an alien audience, they form a bond and ignite a longing for freedom. Together, they plot their escape, daring to dream of returning to their lives on Earth. As they navigate their captivity and fight for autonomy, they are tested but remain unbroken, driven by the hope of weaving their experiences back into humanity's story.

WHISPERS IN THE SAND

Amidst the whispers of the sand and the caress of the Autumn sea, a tale of survival unfolds on the shores of a forsaken island. Here, young Selene and her father carve out an existence, relying on the embrace of nature and each other. Their bond, once threatened by tragedy, burgeons under the trials they face in this barren refuge. But when the island yields an unexpected reunion, the fabric of their family is woven together once more, painting a poignant portrait of hope and resilience. In the cool embrace of a late afternoon's breeze, Selene's heart finds solace, and together, they etch a new beginning upon their souls—an indelible whisper in the fabric of time.

TYLORIN

In the oppressive kingdom of Eldaf, where elves endure human cruelty, a desperate elf mother and her child find an unexpected ally in a compassionate human. Together, they embark on a perilous escape through secret paths and natural sanctuaries, aided by the whispers of the forest's denizens. Their journey leads them to an abandoned, tranquil cottage, where they begin a new life of resilience and love. United by courage and kinship, their bond transcends blood, offering hope and peace amidst the shadows of their past.

ECHOES OF LAUGHTER, ECHOES OF FEAR

In an abandoned amusement park reclaimed by nature, five young explorersâ€”three girls and two boysâ€”embark on an adventure filled with mystery and spectral intrigue. Amid peeling paint and rusting rides, they delve into the park's hidden sorrows, blending nostalgia with a sense of foreboding. As they confront both the park's secrets and their own fears, their journey becomes a test of courage, friendship, and the human spirit. In this eerie yet captivating odyssey, the line between joy and darkness blurs, leaving them to discover whether their bonds can light the way through the park's enigmatic shadows.

SEA OF SHADOWS

Stranded on a solitary island, young Helene navigates a journey of survival and self-discovery, guided by the wisdom of her late father and the lessons of the untamed wilderness. Amid the island's deceptive tranquility, she transforms grief into resilience, building a sanctuary from remnants of the past and forging a future shaped by love and fortitude. Through hardship, Helene finds strength in enduring connections, her father's presence ever a guiding light. Her odyssey is one of emotional catharsis and renewal, where each dawn heralds the triumph of hope and the radiance of new beginnings.

Enchanted Citadel

In a realm where magic and technology intertwine, a group of elite space voyagers embarks on a perilous quest to recover the Chrono Crystal, an ancient gemstone vital for stabilizing the magical streams of their soaring sanctuary, the Enchanted Citadel. As they traverse vibrant yet conflicted planets, they face arcane guardians and looming threats of a malevolent siege. Amidst a cosmic battlefield where starships glide on waves of sorcery and science, the voyagers grapple with unity and betrayal, illuminating paths once hidden in the shadows.

Time has stopped

In *Time Has Stopped*, Elara and her band of weary travelers navigate an endless red desert, a harsh landscape that was once ruled by oceans and now conceals the secrets of a long-lost, water-bound civilization. Battling scorching heat, deceptive mirages, and unforgiving storms, their journey leads them to a colossal statue and an underground labyrinth echoing with the remnants of a forgotten world. Along the way, they form an unlikely bond with a mysterious creature whose loyalty may be their only hope for survival. As the desert tests their resilience and courage, each step comes with sacrifice, forcing them to confront how far they are willing to go to survive the relentless sands of time.

Starborn

In a distant cosmos, the crew of a valiant starship embarks on a perilous journey through the galactic veil, uncovering relics of the ancient Starborn civilizationâ€"artifacts of immense power and potential ruin. As they navigate celestial ruins and decipher esoteric transmissions, the explorers grapple with internal tensions and looming cosmic adversaries. Each discovery brings them closer to revolutionary breakthroughs while risking catastrophic consequences. Caught between enlightenment and oblivion, their odyssey becomes a profound reflection on the morality of progress and the price of knowledge, weaving a tale of human resolve amidst the vast, enigmatic expanse of the stars.

Tales of the Unknown

Word in the forest was that something wasn't right and the creatures were on edge and the slightest noise or movement made them run for cover. Word of this came to Sanction while he was foliage for food. A wagon rolled up and tossed a young girl child from it, she was wrapped inside a burlap potato bag and was tossed aside like trash. Child please dry them tears for you are safe in my forest, like I said no harm will come to you. She sits up and listens to his every word.

Jake found himself enjoying the solitude of the open road. That is, until his car started to sputter. A sudden jolt, leaving Jake stranded in the middle of nowhere. Desperate for help, Jake decided to head towards the building, hoping to find a phone or someone who could assist. Soon to find he has entered where time had stopped and the souls of who where left behind needed to be saved.

Whispers in the Sand

Amidst the whispers of the sand and the caress of the Autumn sea, a tale of survival unfolds on the shores of a forsaken island. Here, young Selene and her father carve out an existence, relying on the embrace of nature and each other. Their bond, once threatened by tragedy, burgeons under the trials they face in this barren refuge. But when the island yields an unexpected reunion, the fabric of their family is woven together once more, painting a poignant portrait of hope and resilience. In the cool embrace of a late afternoon's breeze, Selene's heart finds solace, and together, they etch a new beginning upon their souls—an indelible whisper in the fabric of time.